INTERESTING STORIES

I TOLD MY CHILDREN

FEYI OLUWASANMI

FEYI OLUWASANMI

All enquiries to be directed to the author at:
oluwasanmifeyi@yahoo.com
christimagefoundation@yahoo.com
WhatsApp: +2348067168763
Cover Design: Hadar Creations
Interior Design: Hadar Creations
Publisher: Hadar Creations
WhatsApp Publisher at: +353899465271

ISBN: 978-1-7398826-1-7

Table of Contents

PREFACE

It is evening in Maiduguri, the Borno State capital city in North East Nigeria and my children have just had their dinner. We sit together beneath the yellow sky turning grey and listen to the rhythm of the dusk; families retiring for the day, night insects coming out to duty, the hustle and bustle of a busy day dwindling into a comforting silence and the gentle evening breeze softly piercing our bodies.

The children's brains are probably relaxing from rigorous hours of studying and their nerves calmed by the warm embrace of their humble home. There is nothing better to accompany such adorable twilight than tales from a repertoire of timeless wisdom nuggets from a beautiful magical universe in my imagination.

"Come around, let me tell you a story", I call out. So, the children lay in different positions with their heads on my bare chest. They settle down to a complete silence while I relay interesting folklores to them; wonders of the animal world depicting human relationships, fables with intriguing characters, folk songs and dance rhythms, lessons that would remain with them for the rest of their lives. I teach them about morals and godly behavior –like every responsible parent should.

Some of these folklores I heard or read about, and others I created to address social issues, aided by teachings from the Holy Book. This moment and many more through the years have been fashioned to establish a strong relationship between me and my children. Hence, I have decided to share them with you in this book.

The book, **"Interesting Stories I Told my Children"** is a means of sharing the deep relationship I had with my children as they grew. My excitement at the privilege of being a vehicle through which precious lives will come to the world is inestimable. I was able to impact on the young minds of my children what things the Creator requires from us all, as we navigate this boisterous sea of life.

Consequently, My aim is to make this available to so many other children all over the world; to help parents tap from the well of wisdom and to synthesize rare bonding of love between parents and their children; as well as teachers and their students, so that the family and the nation at large can have a better society where peace and justice and equity reigns.

Africa has a rich deposit of moonlight tales and short anecdotes which are easy to commit to memory and recall when occasion demands. Therefore, I recommend this book to schools, juvenile counselors, social workers, and children.

DEDICATION

I dedicate this book to my children; Seun, Damilola, Ibukun and Ayanfe. I love you so much.

I thank God for blessing me with such godly and goodly children. We surely have our times of differences and challenges. But friends are great, family is best.

I also dedicate this book to The United Nations International Children's Emergency Fund (UNICEF) - the organization saddled with the task of providing humanitarian and developmental aid to children all over the world.

Join me as we navigate the world of folklore and learn some basic truths and principles from them.

ACKNOWLEDGEMENT

To Oluwaseun Kolade Ayodele and Joshua Akinsola for their support in the initial editing work of this book.

To Odun Ofere and Ayodeji Falaye for the painstaking effort in fine-tuning editing and for offering helpful hints.

To all those who helped bear the burden, like Lawrence Alaba Afere and Victor Bamidele Adeyemo

To you, my reader, a partner to this vision

To my wife and children who believe in me.

To Oluwatosin Arodudu for encouraging words and commitment to seeing this get to the foremost parts of the earth.

Spencer John. A worthy team member.

To God Almighty for giving me undeserved opportunity and grace.

AMOPE

Amope; a wealthy woman who once lived in the land of Oleyo, had a violent temper and fiery tongue. Frequently, she picked up fights with neighbors and quarreled with co-traders at the village market and this brewed so much disagreement between her and her husband; Adekoye.

In the home, her husband often got a share of her constant fury, even after the village elders had tried to help. Consequently, he had become exasperated. Whenever they had a disagreement, Amope would play the victim and blame him for whatever misfortune she encountered at the market.

Sometimes, her husband would apologize to her for peace to reign, but she would flare up and continue hurling words at him till she was satisfied.

"But for my children, I would have left this miserable man I call my husband, long ago," Amope told one of her friends, Olabisi who paid her a visit one day. They sat in her living room talking about their businesses and families. "I am sure he is the source of some of my losses at the market. He nags too much," she said.

Olabisi suggested that she visits a traditional healer in the neighboring village of Ayeloro, who could offer her a solution. Amope then decided to pay a visit to the traditional healer in Ayeloro across the *Odo-Ijinle* River, without informing anyone except Olabisi. Since Ayeloro was quite distant, the trip took her almost a day to go and return.

The medicine man's hut sat in the outskirt of the village where he lived like a hermit. Amope got to the hut and offered the wise man some money to homage to his gods.

"Old one, I am unfortunate to have gotten married to a terribly wicked man as a husband," she told him after he gave her a mat to sit and asked why she was in his hut.

"Every day he picks quarrels with me. All I have tried to solve the problem has failed; I am tired of him, Old one. Had it not been for my three children I would have left him."

'So, what exactly do you want me to do, woman?"

"Old one, I need a magic portion to make him do what makes me happy and contented."

The wise man was silent for some time and finally spoke after clearing his voice.

"Are you prepared to make your husband obey you every time?" he said

"Yes" she replied

"You want me to prepare a magic portion for you that will make him do whatsoever you want?"

"Of course!"

"You will have to return tomorrow after the cock crows."

"Alright old one, I will do anything as long as it will help me get my husband to make me happy."

She thanked the wise man and returned to her home in Oleyo. As she approached her compound, she sighted her husband afar off, cross-legged and looking upset.

"Where have you been to since morning, Amope?" He bellowed.

"Where did you send me? Do I not have the right to go anywhere I wish?" She hissed and stormed off.

The next morning, Amope left for the traditionalist's hut in Ayeloro, again without informing anyone. He had been expecting her and she had barely settled down when he began to speak.

"There is a spell on your husband, woman!"

"I know that already, Old one and that is why I have come to you"

"I have all we need to break the spell, but one is left, which you must get yourself."

"I am prepared Old one, what is it?" Amope was getting impatient

"Pick the calabash near the wall, and with it, fetch me fresh milk from a lioness."

Amope gasped, "Did I hear you say the milk of a lioness?"

"Yes, that is the only remaining item to complete the ritual. If you need the solution to this problem, there is no other way"

"But Old one, I have plenty of goats, will their milk not do?"

"No woman, it will not. Nothing will do except the milk of a lioness. A person may have to get to where he'd rather not be before getting to his destination. You must remember, woman; to face war and not flee is the honor of a man"

Amope picked the calabash and left sorrowfully without thanking the man. As she walked home, she cursed her husband for bringing such task upon her. She got to her house and quietly entered her room.

Then she remembered Odenla, the famous hunter who was reputable for hunting and killing several wild games in the past. He became legendary since he started following his father who himself was a great hunter, into the jungle. He also seemed to know every part of the vast jungle. He was well respected for his bravery. Immediately, Amope left for Odenla's compound.

Odenla was relaxing in his compound when Amope arrived. He was surprised to see her. What could have brought such virago to his house, he thought to himself.

"Amope? What a shocking surprise! What can I do for you?"

"Ah ah, Odenla, I was just passing by, and I decided to pay homage to a great hunter," She lied. At this, Odenla erupted in a coarse laughter. Amope was thinking of the best way to introduce the matter without raising any suspicion.

"Can you tell me about lions please? I am certain you must have seen one or two in the forest."

"Lions have great claws and powerful paws. Lionesses are more dangerous to deal with than their male counterparts.

They could be very deadly and ruthless when provoked especially when they have cubs. Usually, a lioness can have about three or four cubs and Cubs are not usually weaned until after two and half months."

"Do you know anywhere in the forest where a lioness just gave birth to cubs?"

"Yes, but why are you asking me all these questions. I hope you are not trying to join the hunters' cult?" He teased.

"No" replied Amope, "I am only curious about the animal world."

"Yes, I know a lioness that just had about two or three cubs, far in the forest" Odenla said, and described the exact location where the lioness who just delivered some cubs lived.

That evening, Amope hurriedly went to the forest judiciously following Odenla's directions. She was able to find the lioness and her cubs just like he had told her. She watched unnoticed by the lioness from her hiding place for some time. The lioness was lying lazily on the grass with three cubs playing around her.

The following day, Amope returned early with slaughtered meat and headed for the forest and the lair of the lioness. From a hiding place, she threw a large chunk of meat towards the lioness. She watched carefully until the lioness withdrew to a ledge then she returned home. She became very tired and took a nap.

The following day, she prepared her chunk of meat and left for the forest again. This, she repeated for two additional days. Meanwhile at home, her husband noticed the insult, affront, and rudeness he often received from Amope had reduced.

This is because by the time she returns from the forest, she would have been tired and would need to get some rest. She would later prepare the meat for the next day's trip to the lion's lair and that was the only task she performed every day.

Amope threw meat at the lioness until she was sure that the lioness was acquainted with her. When she remembered that Odenla told her that lions do not kill for the fun of it, she made up her mind to come to the open. "I can do it," she would keep telling herself to stay encouraged, in the face of such an enormous risk.

After some time, Amope with great trembling came out from her hiding place and showed herself to the lion who had gotten used to getting free meal from nowhere at a particular time every day.

At first, the lioness gave a loud grunt with barred yellowish fangs; but seeing and sensing that the woman standing before her does not mean evil, she backed off and calmed down blinking her eyes.

Amope was elated and threw another chunk of meat towards the lioness before she went back to her home. On the way back, she breathed a sigh of relief and smiled excitedly to herself. The lioness seems to now recognize her as a benefactor and the source of the free meal she had been enjoying in the last few days.

She went to feed the lioness for two other days; only this time, she did not have to hide. The lioness had found a new friend. Even the cubs played around Amope. Gently, she would stroke the mane of the wild animal and whisper to her ears.

On the third day, Amope prepared the meat for the lioness and also took along the calabash that the wise one gave her. She walked straight to the lioness who herself walked majestically to welcome her, shaking her brown tail.

She threw a chunk of meat at the lioness and her cubs, which were now playing around her. Amope began to gently rub her hands over the body of the beast, muttering the words, "I can make it" to herself. With great trepidation, she began to milk the lioness, slowly at first, then with a little more vigor.

All along, the lioness and her cubs were enjoying the large food brought to them. At last, Amope had gotten enough milk and she ran her hand over the animal.

She carefully took the calabash and said farewell to the lion before leaving. She walked and ran, crossed the *Odo-Ijinle* river faster than ever before. She ran until she got to the traditionalist with excitement.

"I made it, Old man, I made it!" She screamed with ecstasy.

"What is it, woman?" the man asked, astonished by such unexpected visit late in the evening.

"The lioness' milk! The lioness' milk!" She screamed as she stretched forth the half-filled calabash to the man.

"How did you do it?" The traditional healer asked. He was shocked as he stared at the calabash in disbelief.

Amope relayed the account of her incredible adventure to the old man. By this time, some neighbors had gathered to hear the reason for Amope's excitement. Everyone was listening with rapt attention to what she had to say, such that one could have heard a pin drop.

The wise man sighed and said solemnly, "Wisdom and patience are required to take an elephant into the city. I congratulate you for the feat that you have accomplished, Amope. You have done the almost impossible, the type that not even the strongest hunters have ever accomplished. If you can milk a lioness, you can live peaceably with your husband and the people around you. Good character is superior to any good luck charm. It is a little quantity of oil that mars the surface of water. You have conquered impatience and arrogance." With that he handed back to her the calabash of milk.

Amope was surprised. She became sober. Her excitement deemed as she walked back home, she pondered over the events of the past days; she could have been killed by the lioness. Rather than prepare for her a charm, the traditionalist had taught her a life-long lesson she would never forget.

Moral Lesson

- **The wisdom required to acquire a house, is nothing compared to what is required to live in it.**

THE LION WHO WILL NOT KEEP HIS PROMISE

O nce upon a time, in the Forest of Wild Leaves, diverse animals and miracles of nature, a powerful lion strolled in the forest. He just had a meal and so was happy with himself; beating his chest as he eulogized himself.

Blinded by the magic of the moment, he fell into a deep ditch. He struggled to come out, but the more he made the effort, the more he fell. With the heavy rainfall the night before, the walls of the pit had become slippery, and the lion slithered down at every attempt to climb out.

By the second day, he had grown weak and tired, exhausted from trying to save himself. Then, he heard the thumps of a buffalo passing, and cried for help:

"Help me out of this ditch, my big friend. I've been here since yesterday." The buffalo stopped and peeped in, and when he saw it was the lion, he replied:

"No! I may be big in size, but I do not have the strength to lift you out of there." So, the buffalo hurried along as fast as his legs could carry him and left the lion there.

Soon, a brightly colored parrot named Majala, flew down and perched on the tree just over the ditch. When the lion saw Majala, he said,

"Help me my friend, l am hungry. I have been here since yesterday and there's no one to help me"

Majala laughed and mimicked the helpless king of the forest in sheer mockery:

"Oh, sorry dear, I cannot help you. I am only a bird with wings remember." So, Majala the parrot flew away and told some animals to avoid going past where the lion had fallen into the ditch.

The following day, Penelope, the giraffe came clopping along the road and met the lion struggling frantically to come out of the pit. The lion was in a pitiable and pathetic condition.

"Oh, my tall friend, please do all you can to bring me out of this problem," the lion cried out to her. Penelope smirked and replied, "Serves you right, old proud lion of the jungle," and left the lion.

The lion remained there for several days and became so emaciated that he looked sad and gaunt.

The following day, Kongi, the monkey hopped along, looked into the pit, and saw the lion lying tired and starved inside the pit. By now, He was moaning in pain finding it hard to breathe properly. The lion raised his eyelids, saw the monkey, and said wearily:

"Oh, my friend, help me out of this hole... I have fallen here for several days... and... and no one wants to help me out... Please do anything to get me out before I die... in this pit..."

Kongi sighed, thought deeply, and asked, "Will you not tear me up and eat me if I help you out of this pit?"

"Why will I even think of a thing like that? I will rather serve and protect you as long as you are in this forest all the days of my life... If you help me now, I will help you when you need help"

"Do you promise me?"

"I promise... I promise... on my honour."

With that, Kongi the monkey made a rope from vines and twines and tied them to a tree. He then let the rope into the ditch and told the lion to hold the rope as he would pull out. The lion wearily did as he was told with the little strength remaining in him. After some hard effort, the lion was pulled out. He breathed fresh air and said quietly to himself, "free at last".

No sooner than the lion was helped, he held Kongi by the throat so tightly he could hardly breathe.

"What are you doing my friend? You are hurting me. I can't breathe," Kongi muttered.

"Don't you know that I have been starving for four days now? I'm really hungry and I will have to eat you to gain some strength to hunt for a bigger prey," the lion said and laughed hysterically. Kongi quickly reminded him of the promise he had made. The lion smiled wryly and told him bad things happens to good people too. Kongi, the monkey wrestled with the lion as he pleaded for mercy over his life.

Unexpectedly, Sarah; the tortoise came crawling along and saw the monkey pleading for his life and weeping. He had gotten news of the lion's dilemma from Majala, the parrot.

"Sorry for intruding on your conversation, what happened?" asked Sagah, the tortoise

Both animals told their own sides of the story; the lion talking of how terribly hungry he was and needing to eat, and Kongi the monkey telling of how he had helped the lion out of the pit with the promise of being repaid for the kindness.

The tortoise then interrupted, "You mean an animal as big as this can enter into this pit? The monkey must be a liar. A lion this big cannot be trapped in this shallow ditch. I cannot believe this"

"Truly I was trapped here, the monkey is right," replied the lion.

"The lion is right to devour you," Sagah the tortoise faced the monkey. "But before I finally conclude on this issue, we have to start from the beginning. I need to see how things were before you caught the monkey." So, the lion demonstrated how he was walking along, boasting, and praising himself and then jumped into the pit.

"You see, the pit can contain me," he said. "Are you now convinced that I was in here for four days?"

Sagah, the tortoise laughed and said, "Old lion, the monkey trusted you and saved your life. You rewarded him with treachery and deceit. After the melon had been used to eat pounded yam, its peelings now became offensive.

You cannot be relied upon, old lion. Now it is your turn to ask for mercy again. Monkey, you may run off and get something to eat. You deserve it. Kongi; the monkey, thanked the old tortoise for saving him from death and then disappeared into the forest. Sagah; the tortoise, laughed out and crawled away, leaving the lion to keep wailing, roaring, and pleading for mercy.

A few days later, Majala the parrot brought news to the tortoise that the lion died in the pit that morning.

Moral lessons

- **Keep your promises**
- **Do not be proud, boastful, and full of yourself**
- **Keep a good relationship with the people around you.**

THE LESSON THE TORTOISE TAUGHT HIS FRIEND

Sagah; the tortoise and Kongi; the monkey were very close friends. They shared so many good things together, supported one another in times of trouble. All the other animals knew that, when you touch one, you touch the other. They ate together and shared their experiences together.

They watched out for one another all the time. While the monkey would assist his friend to get fruits that are high up the treetop where the hands of the tortoise could not reach, the tortoise, being a very clever animal, helped the monkey to get out of difficult problems and challenges. Their relationship grew in leaps and bounds until one fateful day.

The two friends were walking side by side one day when Sagah; the tortoise said, "Terrible things are happening in the forest nowadays. Can you imagine that animals are getting into trouble for what they know nothing about?"

FEYI OLUWASANMI

"Yes," Kongi the monkey replied, "I cannot agree less."

"May God protect us from getting into life's trouble for which we know nothing." Sagah said. There was no reply from Kongi. Instead, he just changed the topic and started a discussion on the varieties of banana that exist in the jungle and how distinctively sweet each one could taste when eaten with groundnut. Sagah considered this action very offensive but decided to keep silent.

The following day again Sagah said to his friend, "This jungle is becoming very dangerous. The reality of injustice is starring us all in face." Again, Kongi showed no concern and Sagah was upset at the kind of response his friend gave to his words. The monkey merely strutted along the bush path as though he had heard nothing. So Sagah decided to bring up the conversation in another way. He continued,

"...and there seems to be nothing that the weaker animals can do about the sad occurrence, we should all be praying for divine protection from evil," He only heard the rustling of leaves in the trees.

The tortoise continued, "May God protect us all from unexpected troubles of life"

"I think we should go to the pond and get some water to drink. It's a sunny day and I'm really thirsty," Kongi said.

The old tortoise could not understand why his prayer for their collective security was not of any interest to his bosom friend. They got to the pond, drank water, and started to return home; meanwhile the tortoise could not stop pondering, thinking of a good time to find out why his friend was behaving so strangely. Therefore, he made up his mind to confront his dear friend on his failure to respond "Amen" to all the prayers he had been offering.

The following day, Sagah; the tortoise purposely reintroduced the matter once more. "May God almighty, the protector of the weak and the vulnerable deliver us from matters of tirade life that come upon us suddenly for which we know nothing about," he stated, and once again, Kongi; the monkey kept silent.

"Dear friend," the tortoise began the tirade, "I have been informing you about the recent disturbing incidences in our part of the forest and you have ignored me, snubbed me or changed the subject matter every single time. What exactly is the reason for this?"

The monkey laughed loud and long until the tortoise became embarrassed. "How could you imagine that such evil will happen to me in this forest? Can't you see my strong arms? Those prayers you made are for sluggish and weak animals not for agile ones like me," the monkey said, holding on the branch of the nearest tree around them and before the tortoise knew it the monkey was high up the treetop, laughing hysterically.

Sagah; the tortoise decided to teach the arrogant monkey a lesson he would always live to remember. He told his wife to fry him some bean cakes mixed with groundnut butter. Then he coated each ball of bean cake with honey. He carefully wrapped them in *"ewe eran"* leaves and went in search of Sandari; the tiger.

It was a tedious search before he found the big strong tiger under the African star apple tree. He approached Sandari and gave him one of the well packaged honey coated bean cake balls. It was unlike anything the tiger had ever tasted and he was curious to know how a slow and relatively weak animal like the tortoise could find so tasty a meal than himself.

"Where did you Sagah get this kind of bean cake balls with your feeble arms, tiny head, sluggish feet and rough shell?" Sandari; the tiger asked. The only answer the old tortoise offered was to give him another of his honey coated bean cake balls.

"Old Tortoise!" The tiger bellowed as he gulped down the balls, "I said, where on earth did you get this kind of meal?"

"This is top secret information. I cannot reveal it to you." Sagah the tortoise replied,

"Please, tell me and I will never reveal it to any animal in this forest. I assure you I am a keeper of my words."

Then the tortoise whispered to him, "This is some of Kongi, the monkey's dung."

"Did I hear you say dung?"

"Yes, of course," replied the tortoise, "You heard me right."

"This cannot be true because I have seen some of monkey's dung on the forest grounds and it doesn't look anything like this."

"Oh" replied the tortoise, "These are special ones which don't come easy. Because it is highly priced and valued, the monkey doesn't release this kind freely unless one pounds, thumps and hits his tummy several times and commands him to excrete them by force."

"Oh, is that so?"

"Yes, I spent a lot of energy to get a hold on these few ones."

The tiger was in a haste to get more of the honey coated bean cake, so he ran off. The tortoise screamed after him, "Make sure you grip him so tightly he cannot escape or else you will not get any sugar-coated bean cake."

Sandari; the tiger then embarked on a frantic search for Kongi; the monkey. He combed through the thicket and the undergrowth. He searched the waving trees and the gentle streams. He kept vigil near the plantain trees and pawpaw trees. Nothing else mattered more to him than getting the honey coated bean cakes.

At last, on one fine afternoon, he caught a glimpse of Kongi and sprang on him all of a sudden. He held him by the thigh as the monkey struggled to escape. The tiger was not only strong and muscular; he was determined to ensure that his prey did not get away. He would not allow the monkey off his grip until he got his honey coated bean cake balls.

"Oh Sandari! How have I offended you this day!" the struggling monkey whined. All that the tiger said to him was to provide his dung. Then he threw a vicious punch at his stomach. The poor monkey winced in pain.

"What on earth have I done to deserve this? Why did I come into this part of the forest today?"

"Kongi, give me the sweet dung!" Sandari screamed at him and threw him another heavy punch. The pain became so unbearable that the monkey was forced to pass out waste by all means. This, he thought, will be better than enduring such pain from the fists of the ferocious tiger.

Without relaxing his grip on the monkey, the tiger took a little bit of the dark, slimy monkey dung and tasted it. It had a bad stench and tasted very bitter and disgusting unlike the one he ate with tortoise. The tiger became so furious and pounded the monkey until he fainted.

Disappointed and sad, the tiger walked away, leaving the monkey swollen, bleeding and broken on the ground. When the monkey managed to wake up, he crawled home, in excruciating pain. He could not understand what he had done to deserve such great deal of violence from the tiger.

The following morning, Sagah; the tortoise paid him a visit at home. Seeing that Kongi the monkey was in a terrible state, he expressed his shock and asked his friend why he looked so battered. The monkey tearfully explained his ordeal with Sandari; the Tiger; speaking slowly and faintly as his head throbbed heavily.

"Why did you not jump on the tree and go high up?" asked Sagah; the tortoise.

"I made attempts, but he was stronger than me," he sobbed.

The tortoise then quipped and prayed, "May God not permit evil we know nothing about to come upon us." Instinctively, the monkey started saying "Amen... Amen... Amin... Amin" and he still says it till this day.

FEYI OLUWASANMI

"Prayers are better than curses; if a prayer is not more than the tip of the fingernail, it is better than a basketful of curses," Sagah the tortoise added.

Moral lessons

- **Do not trust in your own strength.**

THE FOOLISH LION

Mumbu; the lion lived in a forest. He had grown so old he could no longer run as fast as he used to. As days went by, it became more and more difficult for him to hunt and feed.

One day, as he was out searching for food, strolling through the forest, he came across a cave. Peeping inside, he sniffed around the cave and said to himself "An animal must be staying here." On entering the cave, he found it totally empty.

"I will hide inside and wait patiently inside this cave until the animal living inside returns and then I will have some meal," he decided.

The cave was the home of Kiloku; the fox, who had gone out in the morning to hunt and would return to sleep in the evening. As the fox came near the cave after the day's hunting. Suddenly, his instincts told him that something was definitely wrong. Everything was deadly quiet. He sniffed repeatedly but could not find a clue.

"Something is definitely wrong today, even all the birds and insects are so silent," he mused.

Slowly and cautiously, he walked towards the entrance of the cave, looking around to sense any danger lurking around the entrance. Then he came up with a plan. He raised his voice and shouted loudly to the cave "Halloo! My good cave... What happened to you today? Why are you so silent?"

 The echo of his howl startled Mumbu; the lion who had stood up, lurking to launch an attack on Kiloku; the fox. Eager and desperate for a meal, he thought to himself, "I think the cave is silent because I am inside it. I should do something fast before the fox notices."

Again, the fox howled, "Halloo! My good cave, why are you so silent? Have you forgotten that we had an agreement? You are supposed to greet me every time I return home. Why, my good cave, are you failing to welcome me back home?"

At this, the lion tried to change his voice and replied, "Welcome back home my friend." Hearing this, the

FEYI OLUWASANMI

birds up the trees chirped loudly and flew away. Kiloku shook with fear, now certain that his life was in grave danger. He knew a lion was inside his cave. He then got a hook and several sharp-pointed sticks and set a trap in front of the cave. He stayed near the cave and called out once more,

"My good cave, are you so tired you cannot come out to welcome me like you used to? My arms are open wide ready for your warm embrace." Immediately, Mumbu ran out of the cave and open his paws to maul down the fox. However, he got hooked in the trap and was unable to get out. Kiloku; the fox called out to the other animals to come watch how the mighty had fallen.

Writhing in pains, Mumbu; the lion knew that he had been tricked. He blamed himself for his foolishness – allowing his desperation to override his reasoning. He had been a bully who fed on the other animals and his terrible ways had caught up with him.

Moral lessons

- **With patience and wisdom, you can save yourself from lots of troubles**

- **The wicked may rejoice for a while, but his day of reckoning will surely come.**

THE TIGER AND THE LITTLE MOUSE

Sandari; the Tiger was walking along the forest one day, when he caught Tana; the mouse by the tail and was going to place it between his sharp teeth. Sensing the impending danger, Tana cried out with his tiny voice,

"Please, let me go! I am the only one left for my parents"

"Why should I? I found a meal and I am going to eat you up," Sandari replied.

"Oh Sandari, why don't you search for a bigger game, I am too small to fill your stomach."

"Yes, I know that I am however determined to manage this meal until I get a bigger animal. Like an antelope or a buffalo."

"Please don't eat me, I may be of help to you one of these days you know. Small creatures can also be important."

On hearing this, the Tiger busted out with rib cracking laughter, "What impudence! How can you possibly help me? You have tiny paws. You have tiny teeth. Even larger animals in this forest know that they cannot offer any help to me."

Still reeling with laughter, Sandari fell to the ground and dropped the Mouse. Since Tana had amused him and made him laugh so much, he decided to let him go and wait for another day.

Some weeks later, Sandari was walking in the forest again and he suddenly got trapped in a huge net. He struggled and struggled but the more he struggled, the more he got stuck inside the net. He roared and roared, but no help came.

In fact, his roar only drove other animals far away from that part of the forest. Some animals were happy that at last, the predator has been caught in a net. The more the Tiger cried for help and struggled, the more difficult it was to get free. Suddenly, Tana; the Mouse came around and saw the great beast in the embarrassing situation.

"Oh Hello, Sandari" the mouse greeted

"Little mouse, please help me out of here, no one is coming to my help."

"Do you remember what I told you before you let me go the other time?"

"Yes, I do" replied Sandari, with his head bowed and a crestfallen countenance," I'm sorry I mocked you with my laughter the other time."

"Well, it's okay. I will help you just as I promised the other day. But you must also promise not to be mean to the animals anymore. The friendlier we are as a kingdom of animals, the better it is for our world."

"Thank you, Tana, I have realized the errors of my mean ways and I promise to change."

With his sharp teeth, the mouse started nibbling at the net. He worked hard, eating the net a little at a time until at last the Tiger was freed. Sandari; the tiger took the little paws of the mouse in its great paws and said "Thank you, little Mouse. Now I believe that little animals can help bigger animals out of trouble. Thank you, little friend."

Moral Lesson

- **Do not look down on anyone despite their present circumstances**
- **Kindness and unity will go a long way in making our world a better place to be**

ADUKE AND ORI- THE CUSTODIAN OF THE BAMBOO FOREST

O nce upon a time, in the land of Lugbamila, Aduke lived with her family. She was a beautiful young girl, but quite mischievous, pig-headed and a handful for her parents. She refused instructions from older and wiser persons, even if it was to protect her own life.

Rather, she would prefer to do that which she was hell bent on doing. Her parents were sad and afraid that she might not end well if she continued that way. Aduke barely assisted with house chores at home and would instead go on silly adventures, especially to the most ridiculous of places.

One day she said to her father, "Baba, I will be going to the Bamboo Forest today."

"Aduke! No! You are not permitted to go to that forest!" her father emphatically stated, he knew how deadly the Bamboo forest was.

"Why not? I am old enough to take care of myself," She replied indignantly.

"Have you not heard that there are dangerous creatures in that forest?"

"Then why haven't I seen any one of them in the village, tell me," She rudely retorted.

"Oh child! They stay within the boundaries of the forest and do not like people coming there. Do you not see that no village hunter goes to hunt for games in that forest?"

"Nevertheless," replied Aduke indignantly, "I will go to anywhere I please, whenever I please."

So, Aduke waited until her father had slept and went into the Bamboo Forest alone. She was captivated by the immense beauty of the trees, marvelous flowers, and the chirping of brilliantly coloured birds. "What a fantastic view!

How callous for someone to deny another this wonderful experience! I could stay here all day. The village is boring!" She said to herself.

Aduke was enjoying herself so much that she did not notice a huge round being gazing at her from behind and salivating. When she turned round, she was face to face with the fearsome creature. She was transfixed to that spot in utter terror.

Before her was a huge round head, no hands, no legs, no hair nor fur and no clothing of any kind. It had large lips and only one bulging eye. Whenever it spoke, it felt as though there was a heavy downpour on the rooftop of a house. Aduke started to shiver. She had never seen a creature like that before. She did not know what to do.

"I am Ori, the custodian of the Bamboo Forest. Who are you? What is your mission? What do you depend upon? Where did you come from? Who created you as abnormal as this? Why are you looking different from me?

Can you fly like an eagle or swim like a tilapia?" the creature grunted. "Are you an alien in this forest? Have I ever met you before? What is your name? Are you trying to escape from me?" it kept bombarding her with questions without awaiting a reply.

Aduke was sweating profusely and shaking like a leaf in the midst of a harmattan wind. An attempt to run away was futile. She screamed for her father, all she heard was the echo of her own voice against the high mountains nearby.

The creature, Ori grabbed her on the right leg with its large lips and dragged her along the forest floor into a clearing where two desolate huts sat. She was bruised all over and began to feel terribly sick.

Ori was a large ball-like creature that simply rolled across the forest so fast, as though it had a sonic effect.

"How dare you come into my territory?" Ori said again, after it had tied her to a tree. "I am going to teach you a lesson you will never forget. Before I eat you up, I will make you my slave for some days," it said and laughed hysterically.

"What is your name? What should I call you? Where are you from?" it repeated, yelling at her. Shivering and stammering, Aduke told him her name and that she came from Lugbamila, leading to the Mayegunle hills. Both her parents were farmers, she added. Ori laughed and began to torture her by beating her with bamboo leaves all over her body except her head.

Aduke wept bitterly and cried for help, calling for her father and mother, but all to no avail. She saw a black ugly toad around the custodian's cave. The toad was silent but kept looking and studying Aduke's every move. It was there as a guard to make sure no captive escaped.

Ori was also a game hunter and everyday he went out to hunt for rabbits and hares in the middle of the bamboo forest. So, Ori untied her from the tree, placed Aduke near the hearth and ordered her to keep roasting the meat he had killed the previous day.

The following day, Ori said to her, "I am going to the farm today to check my traps. You must roast the meat very well till it will be completely dried." Aduke was subtly happy and hoped it would be an opportunity to escape.

As if Ori knew what her thoughts were, he added "don't even think about escaping, the toad is the sentry here and will keep you in this cave till I am ready to eat you." He called the toad and handed him a bamboo flute, then Ori rolled away into the darker part of the forest. Aduke wondered how a mere toad could stop her from escaping from the forest.

A little while after the custodian left, Aduke saw her chance. The toad was sleeping, so she took courage and started running as fast as she could towards the direction of her home. Suddenly, the toad woke and spotted her; picked up the bamboo flute and started playing a shrill and penetrating song on it.

> *Ori, Ori, please hurry, Aduke is escaping*
>
> *Please hurry up and arrive quickly*
>
> *Aduke is escaping*
>
> *Ori has got no arms*
>
> *Ori has got no legs*
>
> *Ori, Ori please hurry, Aduke is escaping.*

As soon as Ori heard the toad's music, it left everything it was doing and whirled as if driven by a whirlwind in pursuit of its captive. It was so fast Aduke could not believe her eyes when she saw it along her path.

"I am Ori, the custodian of the Bamboo Forest. Who are you? What is your mission? What do you depend upon? Where did you come from? Who created you as abnormal as this? Why are you looking different from me? Can you fly like an eagle or swim like a tilapia? Are you an alien in this forest? Have I ever met you before? What is your name? Are you trying to escape from me?" It said.

With that, it grabbed her by her right leg again and dragged her back into the clearance where the toad was eagerly and excitedly awaiting their arrival. That evening, Ori beat the girl with bamboo leaves again all over her body except the head, and she cried profusely.

The next day, Ori announced to Aduke again that it was going to hunt in the middle of the bamboo forest and warned her not to attempt to escape again because it was sure she had intentions of defying it. When Ori left, and the toad slept as usual, Aduke carefully took the bamboo flute and filled the hollow portion with ashes from the fireplace.

She stuck ashes in until she was convinced it wouldn't work again. She carefully placed the bamboo flute in its normal position. Again, immediately Ori left, Aduke started running away. The toad woke up to see the girl on her heels and quickly took the bamboo flute to notify Ori only this time, the flute has been stuffed with ashes.

Before the toad could suck out all the ashes inside the bamboo flute, Aduke had moved very close to the village of Lugbamila. Nevertheless, the toad still succeeded in playing the music:

Ori, Ori, please hurry, Aduke is escaping

Please hurry up and arrive quickly

Aduke is escaping

Ori has got no arms

Ori has got no legs

Ori, Ori please hurry, Aduke is escaping.

Unfortunately, Aduke fell down at the edge of the village and Ori caught up with her and dragged her by the right leg back to the clearance. "I almost got away... I nearly got my freedom," she lamented amidst tears.

"I am Ori, the custodian of the Bamboo Forest. Who are you? What is your mission? What do you depend upon? Where did you come from? Who created you as abnormal as this? Why are you looking different from me? Can you fly like an eagle or swim like a tilapia? Are you an alien in this forest? Have I ever met you before? What is your name? Are you trying to escape from me?"

Ori began to torture her again with bamboo leaves all over her body except her head. The toad then advised Ori to quickly kill the girl since she was giving them so much trouble. Ori agreed and promised to kill her the following day after it returned from hunt.

Then, the next day, Ori was preparing to go hunting again and told Aduke to roast the meat until it returns. The toad was sleeping when Aduke stuffed his bamboo flute with a lot of ashes. This time she added worms and flies and a few pebbles to make it more difficult for the toad to remove.

"I must escape from this evil creature. I must return to my father. I must apologize for my past disobediences," she soliloquized as she added more pebbles. When she was done, she dropped the flute and began to run away.

Aduke ran as fast as she could towards Lugbamila village. The toad saw her and picked up his bamboo flute, but no music came out. Instead, there were delicious worms and flies to eat. After that, the toad was finding it difficult to remove the pebbles and Aduke got away far away from the clearing. At last, the toad removed all the pebbles and stated playing the same shrill music.

Ori, Ori, please hurry, Aduke is escaping

Please hurry up and arrive quickly

Aduke is escaping

Ori has got no arms

Ori has got no legs

Ori, Ori please hurry, Aduke is escaping.

On hearing the music, Ori came rolling with an amazing speed through the bamboo forest. "This time I will kill this girl. This time I must kill Aduke," it grunted angrily. However, Aduke got right into the village running in the direction of her father's house before the custodian of the forest could get to her.

As soon as Ori saw that Aduke had escaped into her home, it gave up the chase and rolled back into the forest, regretting that he had missed a good meal. Aduke got to her father's house and fell before her parents who had grown worried and had begun to mourn her. She apologized for being a stubborn child and promised to turn a new leaf.

Moral lessons

- **The cost of obedience is small compared to the cost of disobedience**
- **Persistence and determination are the keys to victory**

THE DEEP SECRET OF THE GRANDMOTHER FISH

Once in a large river, Lisa the little fish observed that some fishes suddenly disappeared from the river and no one seemed to know their whereabouts thereafter. She also noticed that at the base of that river was the large grandmother fish —no fish was like it.

While other fishes were disappearing mysteriously, grandmother fish was waxing stronger and bigger. Out of curiosity, Lisa approached the giant fish and started a discussion:

"I have noticed that there is no fish as big and old as you in this river. I also found out that all those of your age have vanished from this river. Please tell me your secret," she said. The big fish kept quiet for a long time and finally opened her mouth,

"When I was a little fryer, I noticed the same thing. I found out that healthy fish suddenly disappear from the waters, I saw many left us unexpectedly"

"So, what did you do?" Lisa asked

"I observed that some worms came from the top of the river and that any fish that tried to eat it was never found again. So, I determined that if at any time I become hungry and need worms I would swim to the floor of the river to search for food.

It may be more energy-sapping and the worms may not be easy to come by, but my safety was always guaranteed. If you want to live long as big as I am, then pick your worms deep. The deeper you search, the safer you are and the longer you live. Never look for food at the surface."

"Thank you, grandmother fish,' Lisa replied.

Morals:

- **Never be superficial or trivial in the pursuit of purposeful living. Dig deep** and work hard to get to the place of power and excel in life.

- You must not fail to talk to successful people on your way to the top. No one is an island of knowledge and a sole custodian of wisdom.

- We all have one thing or the other to learn from one another. Our spiritual relationship with God must be deep.

- People who possess some amount of wisdom for solutions and hold the key for entrance into the goldmine you are searching for, will often stay silent until you ask them.

THE TORTOISE AND THE PIG

Long time ago, there lived a tortoise named; Sagah and a pig named; Bama. While the tortoise was poor, the pig was very rich. The pig also always dressed neatly with expensive clothes and looked well fed all year round.

One day, Sagah was in need of some money, so he went to the pig to borrow. Bama said shrewdly, "So you are here to borrow money from me? Are you ready to pay back with interest?"

"I will try my best. As soon as I harvest my crops," replied Sagah; the tortoise.

"When are you going to pay me back? I don't have patience with lazy folks like you."

"At the end of the harvest season. I have a large yam plantation; after I might have harvested and sold all my crops, I will return the money I borrowed from you."

The pig gave the tortoise a loan of five hundred gold coins and the tortoise thanked him and left. He used the money to buy yam seedlings and new hoes for his farm. Everything was going on well and the tortoise was happy about his crops. Unfortunately, a great storm came upon the village and all crops were destroyed, including those of Sagah, the tortoise.

He became very sad and depressed, and so was his wife; Yannibo. They were both filled with deep sorrow. There was no harvest to make, no food to eat, and definitely no way to repay Bama; the pig. All the animals knew that the pig did not take excuses from his debtors; all who borrowed money from him were so careful not to fall into his wrath.

Meanwhile, the arrogant pig lived comfortably in his luxurious house. He knew some of his debtors would definitely not have the money to pay back, and he took delight in taunting them for it. Sagah went to some of his friends for help, but they were equally poor; so, he started thinking of a way out of the pig's trouble, as the end of the harvest period was drawing closer.

On the day Bama was to come for his money, Sagah was seated in his compound looking out. He knew that the pig would certainly ask for his money, including the interest. Bama got well dressed in fine white robes and headed for Sagah's house. As soon as he got sight of the rich pig coming towards his house, the tortoise quickly instructed his wife to turn him over and start grinding some corn on his belly. Yannibo; his wife, quickly did as her husband instructed her.

The pig entered and shouted, "Where is your husband?"

"Oh, our very generous friend, my husband is not at home. He went to fetch some money for someone who he wants to give. He will be back tomorrow sir," replied Yannibo. The pig sighed and thought in his heart that Sagah had gone to get the money for him. He left and promised to return the next day.

The following day, Bama the pig went again to the tortoise's house and met his wife grinding corn on the stone again.

"My husband is not at home today, he is still gathering money for the person he wants to give, come back another day sir," Yannibo said. The pig became upset and returned to his house, running out of patience with the tortoise.

The following day, Bama; the pig came again and met the tortoise's wife grinding corn on the stone.

"I must see your husband today," he grunted

"Oh no, he is not at home, he..."

"Don't give me any excuse. You both think you can dupe me and get away with it? Never!" Angrily, he kicked the grinding stone over the wall without knowing it was the tortoise. "I will be back before long, and you will not like the consequences of my return!" With this, he left furiously again, while at the other side of the wall, the tortoise rolled over and returned to his house.

Bama returned the following day, this time he met both Sagah; the tortoise and his wife, Yannibo.

"You! Where is my hard-earned money?" he bellowed, pointing at Sagah.

"Yannibo; my wife, please get me the money I kept under the grinding stone" the tortoise replied, calmly.

"Oh, I forgot to inform you. The pig came yesterday and kicked the grinding stone over the wall." Yannibo said.

"Is that so, Mr. Bama?"

"Oh Yes. I was provoked," the pig replied.

"Then you had better get me my grinding stone. The money I owe you is under it."

The pig quickly ran out and discovered that the area where the money had supposedly fallen, was filled with mud. So, he entered the mud and started searching for the grinding stone with his snout. He searched and searched but could not find the grinding stone.

At dusk, he returned to his pen grunting sadly after taking a bath. Very early the next morning, he resumed the search all over again but did not find the grinding stone. He is still trying to find it till today; and that is why pigs can be found burrowing through mud puddles, searching for food with their snout.

Morals

- **A stone thrown at a bird in anger cannot kill the bird**
- **Show mercy to the less-privileged around you**
- **As much as possible, avoid anger in all your interactions with people**

THE COCK AND THE FOX

O nce upon a time in the land of the animals, the was a cock named; Gagara, who was well respected and feared amidst all the animals in the kingdom. He had the most brilliant and colorful feathers. Other animals envied his ability to know the time and to awake them with all costae nice voice every morning. But Aburu; the jackal feared the cock more than any other animal. He would avoid him at all cost.

One day, Aburu; the jackal was walking along a bush path when the cock came crowing happily in the opposite direction. The jackal ran into the thicket; he kept running until he could no longer hear the crowing of the cock.

Gagara; the cock took notice that the jackal was always running away from him or avoiding him every time their paths crossed, especially whenever there is a meeting of all the animals in the kingdom. So, he made up his mind to get close to the jackal and make him his friend.

As soon as he walked towards Aburu; the jackal sprinted off as if a thousand devils were after him. The cock was embarrassed and felt very bad.

Yet, he made up his mind to remove Aburu's fear of him and to try and get friendly with him as soon as possible. However, all his efforts proved futile, as the jackal kept shifting farther away each time he tried to speak with him.

One day, the cock followed the jackal to a close end and came near him. The jackal was shivering, but the cock drew closer.

"Aburu; my friend, why do you always run away any time you see me coming near you? Am I so terrible or terrifying?" The jackal started sweating and getting ready to scamper off with high speed,

"Why are you afraid of me?"

By now, Aburu had begun to weep,

"There is no need to cry, Aburu. I am harmless. Why are you so afraid of me?"

Aburu could only point to the cock's head, "because of the flame of fire you always carry on your head everywhere you go."

"Oh" exclaimed the cock, "this is not a flame of fire!"

The jackal was already running away.

"Come back, Aburu! Come and touch it by yourself and see that it is completely harmless. Come closer"

So, the jackal tentatively moved towards the jackal and carefully touched the comb of Gagara, the cock, and confirmed it as cold as ice.

"I did not know that your comb was as cold as that all this while. I was thinking that the red color shows that it is flaming hot and that you are the most dangerous bird on earth," the jackal then left for his home.

The following day the jackal searched for Gagara. He found him picking some grains from the ground. He walked straight to him and grabbed him by the neck and devoured him. Since then, cocks have become the nourishing food for jackals everywhere.

Morals

- **Do not disclose your secret to your enemy**

THE LITTLE BLACK DOG

Some times ago in the land of the animals, there was a long famine. It was so severe that not even a grain of guinea corn was found in the entire kingdom, and animals had begun to die. The younger animals then called a meeting to discuss the issue and find a lasting solution.

"It's the fault of our mothers. They have refused to give us food," the pigeon said.

"They do not love us," added the zebra.

"Mothers are supposed to find food for their young ones, not watch them starve," agreed the lion.

At last, they all consented that they would kill their mothers and eat them all. Every single animal was pleasantly satisfied with that decision, and they began to make plans to carry out their mission.

The little black dog however said to himself, "You do not bite the fingers that once fed you. It is not correct to repay good with evil." So, he went to his mother and said, "Mother, all the animals have agreed to kill their mothers for food because of the terrible famine. They said you mothers were to be blamed. Let's hurry! I am going to hide you in the cloud where the rest of the animals will never see you and hurt you."

So, the little black dog took his mother to the cloud and hid her there.

"You must never tell any of the animals about what happened here today," warned the little black dog's mother, "we must keep it a secret."

Every morning and evening the little black dog will go near a huge *iroko* tree and begin to sing...

> *Mother, my mother let down the rope*
>
> *All other animals have killed and eaten their mothers*
>
> *I hid my own mother in heaven.*
>
> *Mother, my mother let down the rope*

As soon as he finished singing, a very long rope with a basket at the end would come down from the cloud and the dog would jump into the basket and be pulled into clouds. While in the cloud with his mother, the dog would eat and drink and return to the earth. He would also tell his mother whatever was happening in the animal kingdom.

This continued daily. Meanwhile, the other animals had finished eating all the meat of their mothers and were hungry again. Once again, the famine came upon the land and there were no more mothers.

The animals started regretting their action against their mothers and some started realizing that the famine was not the fault of their mothers after all. The famine seemed to be more terrible than before the animals killed and ate their mothers. While the rest of the animals were getting thinner and thinner, the little black dog was growing fatter and fatter.

The old tortoise: Ijapa, soon noticed that the dog was not losing weight like himself and other animals in the kingdom and he became curious and started nosing around. One day, he paid a visit to the little black dog's kennel.

"How is life with you? The famine is killing almost every animal in our kingdom, but you are looking healthier and well fed in spite of the famine, my friend," he said. "A man with one bad eye is seldom thankful to God until a speck enters the good eye. We made a big mistake by blaming our mothers for the famine. I did not notice you killing your mother, my friend."

"But the decision we all took was that we should all kill our mothers. You were in the meeting, Ijapa," the little dog replied.

Ijapa then left the little dog's kernel quietly, but his curiosity only grew. He knew there was something secretive about the little black dog. Therefore, he started spying and secretly following the dog around. One day, he was hiding under a rock to spy on the dog, when he heard the dog singing his song

> *Mother, my mother let down the rope*

> *All other animals have killed and eaten their mothers*

> *I hid my own mother in heaven.*

> *Mother, my mother let down the rope*

The little black dog had barely finished when the old tortoise, with dropping jaws, saw a basket at the end of the rope. He saw the dog jump inside. He saw the rope being pulled back into the clouds. Ijapa ran quickly to the rest of the starving animals and told them what he had seen. The animals were upset and considered the little black dog, a traitor. Then, Ijapa suggested that they all go to the sky to eat the mother dog, and they all agreed. So, he led all the other animals to the spot behind the big *Iroko* tree and started singing:

> *Mother, my mother let down the rope*
>
> *All other animals have killed and eaten their mothers*
>
> *I hid my own mother in heaven.*
>
> *Mother, my mother let down the rope.*

As the other animals watched, the long rope came down and all the animals rushed into it with knives, clubs, and stones; the monkey, hippopotamus, the lion, the tortoise, the antelope and the hyena, the elephant, and the giraffe, they all climbed into the basket and the basket started to move away from the earth into the cloud.

Inside the cloud, the little dog's mother noticed that the basket was very heavy. She was struggling to pull it up, so she looked through the cloud window and saw all the animals except her son with weapons. She quickly took a knife and cut the rope, and all the animals came crashing heavily to the earth.

Morals

- **Be respectful to parents and older people, and treat them well for they have made sacrifices for you**
- **Do not follow the crowd of people to do wickedness and show cruelty to others.**

THE TORTOISE AND THE SNAIL

The tortoise and the snail were both hunters. Very early every morning, the snail would wake the tortoise so they could go check their traps for any game. The tortoise's trap would only catch small rodents, while that of the snail would catch big animals like gazelles, antelopes and large grasscutters. The snail would then sell the game he caught in the village market, and soon became very rich. This happened every day and made the tortoise very sad and jealous.

One day, the trap of the tortoise could only catch a small cricket, and by the time the snail brought his own catch, it was a big warthog. So, he blurted out angrily, "How come you are always catching all the big animals while I catch the small ones or even nothing, sometimes?"

"It is because while I set my trap in the middle of the forest, you always set your own trap very close to the footpath," the snail replied

"How can that prevent large animals from being caught?"

"I have been telling you that big animals do not come to the footpaths. If you want to get bigger game, you must put more effort and move into the center of the forest."

"No! You must have been swapping my catch!" the tortoise retorted.

"No, that is not true. Moreover, you have to get a bigger trap to catch bigger animal. This trap of yours is just too small," the snail explained. But the tortoise was not going to believe the snail. At home he discussed the issue with his wife, and he started hatching a plan.

One morning, the tortoise woke up well before the arranged time, went through the back door and went to the place he set his trap near the footpath, he was not surprised that he caught nothing. He moved quickly to the spot where the snail set his trap and found an antelope.

He gently removed the trapped antelope and took it to his own trap. He carefully fixed the catch in his trap and sneaked back to the village and to his home before the snail came wake him.

No one knew when he left, and no one knew when he returned. When the snail got to his house, the tortoise pretended to be in pains and asked the snail to go alone as he was feeling very sick. The snail was sympathetic; he wished the tortoise quick recovery and left for the forest alone. On getting to the footpath, he saw antelope at tortoise's trap, and he was amazed.

"What a pleasant surprise! Tortoise's trap has finally caught a big antelope!" he said. However, when he got to his own trap, it was empty.

"Some days are like that," he mused. He carried the antelope to the tortoise house and announced "how lucky you are today! Your trap caught an antelope, I'm happy for you," he announced happily.

The tortoise pretended to still be in pains and "Thank you, Oh!! Ah! Yeee! But I'm not strong enough to see you off. Oh!! Ah! Yeee! My stomach! Ah! Yee!"

"It's okay my friend, rest now and get well soon. I have also set both our traps for tomorrow," the snail told him.

Immediately the snail departed for his house, the tortoise stood up; cooked the antelope and feasted.

The next day, very early, the tortoise woke up and headed for the location where he set his trap. Expectedly, he found a tiny rat in his trap. He went to the location of the snail's trap and discovered that the trap had caught a big warthog.

Once more, he took away the warthog and placed it carefully as though his own trap caught the animal and left the snail's trap, empty. Before he was seen by anyone, the tortoise had returned to his home and pretended, as usual, that he had been sick.

As soon as he heard footsteps, he knew that the snail was coming to wake him up; he started groaning as if he was sick and in great pains. The snail wished him quick recovery and left for the forest to help check their traps alone.

He got to the trap of the tortoise first since it was closer to the footpath and was surprised to find in the trap a big warthog. When he got to his own trap right in the middle of the forest the trap only captured a tiny rat.

The snail carried the warthog to the tortoise who ate some and sold some. So, while the tortoise was getting richer and fatter, the snail had nothing to show for all his effort.

This continued for about fourteen days, so the snail one day announced dejectedly to the tortoise that he would no longer set traps but would find a new means of getting income.

"If the quantity of water one has is not enough for a total bath, one should simply use it to wash his face. I have purchased a gun since I have been unlucky with traps for some time now and you my friend have been so sickly of late. I will now hunt with a local gun," he said.

One day, the tortoise went to borrow the snail's gun for hunting. When he got to the forest, he saw an animal on a tree and took aim. He shot and was so delighted at his good aim.

However, on getting closer to the prey, the tortoise found out that it was not a monkey he shot at, but the king's dwarf who was the village town crier. The king was very fond of his dwarf and everyone in the village was well aware of the close relationship between them. The tortoise was scared.

"What am I going to do now? This is real trouble for me. The king is certainly not going to spare anyone who kills his dwarf town crier," he cried silently. He then carefully placed the dead dwarf on the low branches of a tree.

So, he hurried to the snail's house and asked him, "Aren't you going to hunt with your new gun today?"

"No," replied the snail. But the tortoise lured and persuaded the snail to accompany him to the forest. He had carefully placed the dead dwarf on the low branches of a tree. He gave the snail the gun and showed him the target on the tree.

"Do you see the monkey up on the tree?"

"Yes,"

"Since you are a better shot than I am, I will advise you to shoot it before it escapes." The snail shot and down fell the dwarf with a thud. It was not until they got closer to take a better look and to pick up the animal the snail killed, that he realized that it was the king's dwarf and not an average monkey. The snail was in grief.

"Oh no! You have killed the king's dwarf, now you are in real trouble," the tortoise cried. Before the snail could do anything, the tortoise scurried off to invite the other villagers to the scene. "The snail has killed the king's best friend," he screamed.

The mob rushed to the spot and found the snail mourning. So, they invited the palace guards, and the snail was taken to the palace. In anger, the king sentenced him to death and so he was placed in the prison awaiting his execution.

While in prison, the snail started suspecting that something was amiss, so he asked for an audience with the king.

"Kabiesi, will you permit me to give you my last wish. It may help us know who really killed your favorite town crier," then he whispered something into the ears of the royal father.

The next day, the king asked that the snail be dressed in purple *asooke,* and royal beads worn on his neck. He ordered his drummers to sing, dance and conduct the snail throughout the village, singing:

I have killed the Kings dwarf

I have been made a chief

See what luck has brought me

How could I have known that the king has been searching for who will help him kill his town crier.

I have killed the king's dwarf

I have been made a chief.

At home the tortoise heard the sound of music and went to find out what was happening in the village. He listened carefully to the words of the song as the people were singing and dancing happily.

He came out and saw the snail dressed in royal attires, riding upon a horse and followed by drummers and dancers accompanied by a jubilating crowd. The snail was smiling and waving at the crowd and some onlookers were even paying obeisance to him. Little children were running happily alongside the horse, singing:

I have killed the Kings dwarf

I have been made a chief

See what luck has brought me

How could I have known that the king has been searching for who will help him kill his town crier.

I have killed the king's dwarf

I have been made a chief.

The tortoise could hardly believe his eyes. He hurriedly ran to the palace and sought audience with the King and the chiefs.

"Kabiesi, your royal highness, you did not investigate the matter properly before jumping to conclusions. Your Royal highness, it will surprise you, but I killed your dwarf town crier, not the snail. As such, I deserve to be installed the chief," he said.

"That is not possible," replied the king. "The snail killed my dwarf with a gun, and he is the one that is entitled to the chieftaincy title."

"I am the one responsible," insisted the tortoise

"Can you prove it so everyone will know?"

The tortoise then breathed heavily and said, "I was the one who saw the dwarf when I was hunting for game on that fateful day. I took him to be a monkey, so I fired a shot. When I moved nearer, I saw that it was your favorite town crier. Then I did not know you will honor whosoever helped to kill him. So, I called the snail to aim at the already dead dwarf."

There was a hushed silence in the palace at this time. The snail and the throng who followed him on foot were just returning from the village square, and so the king asked tortoise to repeat his assertion. The tortoise boldly repeated his statement and the people shouted in disbelief.

The king explained how he had doubted that the snail was the culprit since everyone knew he was of a noble character and had decided that he should be kept in prison first. He also explained how the snail had come up with a plan to find the dwarf's true killer. The tortoise was sweating profusely, as he realized that he had been caught.

The king then ordered that the tortoise be executed for killing the dwarf and implicating one of the worthy sons of the land. He also ordered that the snail be given a chieftaincy title indeed, as his wisdom had helped to discover the truth behind the abomination that the tortoise had committed.

And so, the tortoise was executed in the palace prison.

Moral lesson

- **Laziness breeds evil. But the hardworking man has no time on his hands to plot evil.**
- **No matter how long evil rules, the truth will eventually triumph.**

THE TORTOISE, THE RAT AND THE SQUIRREL

Once upon a time, the tortoise and the squirrel were good friends selling wares in the village market. The tortoise and the squirrel both sold clay pots. The rat, however, sold palm kernels. The rat and the squirrel had their stalls close to each other. The squirrel loved to eat palm kernel very much, so one day, he took some of the rat's palm kernel without asking.

The matter resulted in a serious argument which led to a fight between the two animals. When the tortoise got to the market later that day, he was informed by some of the animals, about what had transpired. The tortoise left his wares and ran to the place of the fight.

Without asking any questions, he started beating the rat with blows and slaps. The other animal traders were watching with disgust. This is not right, they said to each other.

The tortoise hit the rat on his back and squeezed his arm so tight, that the squirrel got a chance to escape. He hit the rat again and declared that he would not tolerate any brawl between both rodents in the marketplace.

When the rat realized that the tortoise, rather than being a peacemaker or an unbiased go-between, was craftily taking sides with his friend, the squirrel, sank his teeth into the tortoise's nose biting hard in frustration.

"Let me go! Let me go!!" the tortoise cried, but the rat turned a deaf ear and kept holding firmly unto tortoise's nose.

He started appealing to the crowd in a mournful song:

> *The rat and the squirrel were having a fight*
> *I came to stop the fight*
> *I left all my clay pots in my stall*
> *The rat bit off my nose.*
> *Please rescue me from his hands*

But rather than help him, the other animals, knowing what happened, just ignored his appeal, "That serves you right!" they all said. No one moved a muscle to help him until the rat completely cut off his nose. Blood was flowing freely from the nose of the tortoise as he ran back to his stall in pains.

The tortoise nose has remained a small stump after it healed since the day the rat severed it out of frustration. The old tortoise never again was partial or prejudiced.

Moral Lessons

- **Be fair in your judgment and avoid partiality or prejudice.**

THE DEBT OF PAST GENERATIONS

O nce upon a time, a trader named Awofele in the village of Oleyo, went to neighboring villages to trade. He made a lot of profit and was returning home happily with a bag of money. He had never had it so good and was thinking of how he would spend the money and become famous as he walked back to his village through a bush path.

On the way, he had to cross the flowing *Kagbesan* stream and because the sun was a bit scorching, he decided to have a quick bath before resuming his journey. So, he removed his clothes and hung them on the branch of a tree for safety.

The water was as clear as crystal and was inviting. He placed his bag of money inside a vine grass farther away from where he hung his clothes. He then lunged into the river and washed his body; letting the cool water run over him, swimming and playing with water till he was satisfied.

At last, Awofele came out of the stream and put on his clothes, singing happily to himself. He caught sight of a mango tree somewhere in the near bush path and went to pick some ripe, succulent mango fruits and held them in his hands, eating and enjoying it as he walked towards his village.

"Life can never be better," he said to himself, "When I get home, I will certainly show everybody that times have changed for good for me as I will first change the roof of my house. Then, I will marry the most beautiful maiden in the village.

It will be the king's daughter, and so I will be highly respected as the king's in-law in the village and beyond. The rest of my money... money... my bag of money!", when he mentioned this, he looked and discovered that the bag of money was not with him. He threw away the remaining mangoes in his hands and started running back towards the stream.

Meanwhile, when he left the stream, a monkey came to have a drink and found the bag of money where the merchant left it. He opened, started scattering the money into the stream playfully. He threw some into the air and the wind took them very far away. He tore some to piece and used them to wipe his running nose. When the monkey got tired, he went to the stream, drank more water, and returned to the forest.

After this, a young man came to wash in the stream and noticed some of the money sprawling all over the bank of the stream. He looked around; seeing no one, he said "Hello! Is anyone around?" when no one replied, He picked all the money near the bank that have not been washed away by the flowing stream; he caught some flying in the air and picked the bag. The man quickly left the stream, disappeared behind the bushes, and sneaked home unnoticed by anyone.

Shortly after he left, a blind man also came to the stream to take his routine afternoon bath. He had been there to bathe several times in the past. As he was taking off his dresses, and sitting down, the merchant ran into the clearing, panting. The blind man was singing to himself when the merchant suddenly appeared. He swiftly ran to where he kept the bag looked frantically around and did not find it.

"Where is the bag of money here?" he screamed at the blind man

"I don't have an idea of what you are talking about", replied the blind man

"Where have you hidden it, you thief!"

"What are you trying to say? What money are you talking about? Do you not see that I cannot see anything or anyone?"

The merchant did not believe the blind man and he began to wrestle with him. The blind man groped for his walking stick but before he could get it, the merchant gripped his neck and started hitting him all over his body.

"You must produce my money! It is my hard-earned income. Give me back my money, you villain and stop pretending you are blind," the merchant shouted.

"Yay! Yay! I have stolen no money. I don't know about your money!" the blind man cried.

The merchant continued beating the blind man until he slumped, with blood oozing from his left ear and his nostrils. When the merchant realized that he had just killed the blind man, he became afraid and took to his heels.

A gentle breeze blew across the leaves of the trees and the birds chirped near their nests. The grass by the stream seemed to glow brighter than ever before.

Who is guilty?

Some people said that the merchant was at fault. The reason is because He was not careful with his properties. He also could not control his temper. Some laid the blame on the blind man who ventured to the stream without a guide. Still, some blamed the monkey for not allowing other people's properties to be. Others blamed the man, who took away the remainder of the money that the monkey wasted.

Suddenly a spirit appeared and gave a proper explanation to the whole issue:

Once upon a time, the spirit said, *a man called Alonilowo borrowed some money from another so that he could buy some food for his family. He only tricked his benefactor. He collected the money but escaped from the village and the lender could not recover his money till he was killed.*

Alonilowo was the great grandfather of the Awofele, the merchant who forgot his money near the stream;

the money lender was the great grandfather of the man who picked the money by the stream, and the killer of the money lender was the great grandfather of the blind man. That amount the merchant was able to gather was the exact money that Alonilowo owed the money lender, including the interest. The great grandfather of the blind man was the one who murdered the money lender. Therefore, the money had now returned to the lineage of the money lender; taken away from the lineage of Alonilowo, while the descendant of the killer had also been murdered.

The people sighed and agreed to the judgment of the spirit, as they prepared to bury the blind man.

Moral lesson

- **What goes around, often comes around. Posterity will account for whatsoever you do.**

THE KING'S SUCCESSOR

There was once a king named Baderera, and his wife; Abeni, who were barren. They had tried all means to have a child, but none turned out successful. This made the king very worried; he would always wonder who would become the next king when he dies.

He met several herbalists who could not solve the problem. Every day, the problem was weighing him down. But because he loved his wife very much, there was nothing he could do. The queen was known in the village as a very kind and amiable woman.

After much thought and pressure, one day, he decided to marry another wife, Ajitoni, following the advice of one of his closest aides: Chief Bobajiro. Ajitoni decided that if she gets pregnant, she was going to be the only queen in the kingdom.

She got pregnant and gave birth to a daughter. Fortunately, that same month, the older queen, Abeni became pregnant also. Jealous that the senior wife will also have a baby very soon, Ajitoni started to make trouble with her so much so that the king spent a lot of time settling the quarrels between the two women.

One day the older wife cooked some food for the king. Chief Bobajiro suggested that the king would give some of the food to two of his dogs who were lying down beside him.

"My king" said chief Bobajiro, "I will advise that you find a way of testing every food you eat within this palace."

"Why should I do that? I have two loyal wives," the king replied.

"I am only suggesting this in view of the constant quarrels between the two queens in recent times. You can never be too careful you know, *Kabiesi*."

So, the next time the king was served pounded yam with melon soup by the older queen, he gave the dogs some of them. Not too long from then, the two dogs fell down, and later died.

The king was shocked and angry, ad he ordered that she should be taken to the village square and punished.

There was an outcry in the kingdom because the food was cooked and served by the first wife, "She's a witch! She's a witch! Kill her! Kill her!" they all cried.

The king was so disappointed at the behavior of his favorite wife. She insisted that she was innocent and pleaded with the king to investigate the matter patiently. No one could explain why she had to act so shamefully.

The king banished her from the kingdom and ordered that she should never set foot in the kingdom again. The queen was led by a jeering crowd out of village in a show of shame. She wept and pleaded, but no one would listen.

She moved into the forest where she had only animals and wild creatures as companions. She became depressed and sad at how life had treated her. A few months later, she gave birth to a baby boy and named him Aremo; but because she was scared of how the villagers would treat her if she ventured to the village again, she did not take the news to the village.

She nursed the baby carefully from the products of the farm she started by her hut. Sometimes people come around from the adjoining villages either in transit to another village or hunters who came searching for games in the thick forest.

In the process of time, the baby grew to be a young, handsome man with excellent hunting skills. However, in the village of king Baderera, things were not going well. The other wife just got delivered of the fifth girl and the king became highly troubled. "How will I sustain my family name on the throne of my forefathers?

To whom will I hand over the throne? All my children are girls," he moaned continuously and lost his appetite. He refused to see the new baby and refused to give her a name.

King Baderera soon became very sick and was about to give up the ghost. All the best traditional doctors in the kingdom were summoned to prescribe healing herbs for him. However, they saw little or no progress.

One day, two hunters went to hunt and saw Aremo. They were amazed at how he had a striking resemblance to King Baderera. Immediately, they ran to the village to inform Chief Bobajiro of what they had seen. The chief followed the hunters back to the forest and secretly traced the old queen's hut. He became disturbed and greatly worried.

"You must keep this away from the king or anyone for that matter and I will reward you handsomely," he told the hunters.

The hunters were surprised as to why the chief wanted to keep such discovery a secret, however they obliged. The king grew worried every day about his inability to bear a son who would take over from him when he died. One day, one of the village hunters went into the forest to hunt and got bitten by a snake.

Aremo found him and took him home where his mother helped to treat and nurse him till, he was okay. The hunter then thanked Aremo and his mother and promised to repay their kindness someday. He however remarked that Aremo had a striking resemblance with their king even though the king had no son.

Aremo then narrated to the hunter how his mother was wrongly accused and banished by the king years earlier. The hunter then decided in his heart that he would help Aremo, and the old queen get the justice they deserve.

When he returned to the village, he went directly to the king and told him he had a plan of finding the next perfect king. At first, the king was reluctant, but the hunter came back with the village's soothsayer, and they hatched a plan.

The following day, the soothsayer announced that in order for the king not to die, there had to be a feast where the queen would cook him a special delicacy and watch him eat it.

By doing that, he said, the king would live many more years and would bear a son. On the day of the feast, the queen Ajitoni prepared a dish and brought it before the king and the villagers.

However, the king demanded that his daughters should eat out of the food, as he desires to make one of them the next queen. Then, he called his daughters forward to eat it. Immediately, Ajitoni screamed and told them not to eat the food. The villagers were surprised.

They expected her to be happy that one of her daughters would eventually become a ruling queen. The queen refused vehemently, saying her daughters must not eat out of the food. The king then asked his closest friend, Chief Bobajiro to eat out of the food and

FEYI OLUWASANMI

he also refused, saying he cannot eat the food belonging to a king.

Then, the soothsayer said they would be struck dead if they do not begin to confess their evil deeds. The queen Ajitoni then confessed that she connived with Chief Bobajiro to get rid of the senior queen Abeni by implicating her.

She also confessed that she connived with him to get rid of the king by poisoning the food so that Bobajiro would become king. The villagers were shocked at this and disappointed that Bobajiro would betray the trust the king had for him. The king then gave an order that both Ajitoni and Bobajiro be banished from the kingdom immediately.

''Remove the bead from his neck,'' the king ordered his palace guards.

He went with his royal envoy into the forest to search for his beloved wife and son. The villagers apologized to Abeni for the wrong they had done to her and in an honorable procession, Abeni and her son; Aremo were led back to the village. The king gave an order that his son Aremo would be the next king after his death, while the kind hunter would be Aremo's right hand chief.

Moral Lessons

- **No matter how long falsehood reigns, the truth will catch up to it one day**
- **In the company of the wicked, there is destruction and safety in the gatherings of the righteous**

THE ALAGATA COCOA TRADER

In Alagata kingdom, there lived a very hard and stingy man called Owolagba. He was a great merchant selling large amounts of cocoa and kolanut which he inherited from his late father. The man was married to a woman called Olanike. The problem was that he was always unwilling to share his belongings with the needy.

He would rather have the cocoa seed rotten in his store than give it to them. He saved his money everywhere and sometimes forgot where he hid it. "Someone must have stolen my money," he would say, and begin to suspect everyone around him.

Sometimes, he would accuse his wife of stealing from him; sometimes it was his neighbors he accused of stealing his money and cocoa seeds. If he saw another farmer drying his cocoa beans, he would say, "that man must have stolen this from my farm or store. These beans are certainly mine."

FEYI OLUWASANMI

One day, Owolagba misplaced a thousand pieces of gold coins which he tried to hide in a safe place in the bush. Unfortunately, he could not remember the exact spot he hid it. He lost both sleep and appetite, searching frantically for the misplaced items. He ran quickly to the King's palace and lodged a report. He promised to give a reward of one hundred pieces to whosoever found the bag of gold coins.

Then the following day, a poor woman called Iwa was trying to get some firewood to cook the little food remaining in her hut. Suddenly the woman saw something like a bag underneath a shrub. Out of curiosity, she pulled it out and opened the bag.

She was shocked as she saw such an exorbitant amount of gold coins, more than she had ever seen in her life, or dreamed of ever seeing her lifetime. Instinctively, she dropped the bag of gold coins as though she mistakenly held a snake. She ran away a short distance and returned, after gathering enough boldness to pick the bag of cowrie shells again.

Iwa took the bag to her husband and relayed the story of how she found the bag of gold coins to her husband.

"We are rich, we are wealthy!!" her husband screamed.

"No, this is not our money," his wife said firmly. "We must not take other people's belongings,"

"But Iwa, you found it, you didn't steal it."

"And I insist, we must get the money returned to its rightful owner."

"My dear wife, we are facing the storm of starvation, hunger and poverty, and God has answered our prayers by giving us this wealth. Now you want to throw it all away?"

"Yes, the storms of the sea will not stop the fish from sleeping and even snoring," replied Iwa.

They continued to argue without reaching a conclusion, until Iwa left through the backdoor and headed for the palace. Seeing that he could not change her mind, her husband gave up and followed her as they both went to report the found item to the King.

The couple went to the palace and explained exactly what they knew about the bag of gold. The king and the other chiefs were so elated to find an honest woman like Iwa. The king then sent for Owolagba who came hurrying to the palace as soon as he learnt that the king wanted to see him. He met the guests at the palace, and at the king's cue, they explained how they had found the money under the shrub. Owolagba looked at the woman and considered her faded and ragged dress.

"If I give this poor wretched woman and her husband a hundred piece of gold, they will become arrogant, the reward is too much for them. To get a reward of so much gold pieces just like that? She saw my missing bag by coincidence," he soliloquized.

Then he cleared his throat and addressed the king, "This woman must have taken part of the money before reporting that she found the bag. The gold pieces are not complete. She has definitely helped herself to some of them!"

"I did not take any of your money, sir," Iwa replied instantly.

"Yes, you did!"

"How many pieces did you lose, Owolagba?" the king asked.

"I lost one thousand, five hundred pieces your highness. Now what is in this bag is only one thousand pieces, this woman and her husband must have conspired to take five hundred pieces."

"My wife is not a thief, *Kabiesi* and we never conspired to steal any piece of gold."

Then the king said, "Give me the bag and allow me to confirm what you are claiming." Owolagba handed the bag over to the king, who counted and agreed that Owolagba was speaking the truth about the amount he left there.

Then the king said, "Since you had one thousand five hundred pieces and the woman brought a bag containing one thousand pieces of gold, it could only mean that this bag of gold is not the one you lost."

Then, the king gave the bag of gold to Iwa and told her to go home. He turned to Owolagba and said, "You may leave now, whenever we find the bag containing one thousand, five hundred pieces of gold I will definitely send for you."

Owolagba bit his fingers as he left the king's palace. He tried to think of a means to get the money back, but he could not. He went home in regret and never got his missing bag of gold.

Moral lesson

- Honesty is a necessary virtue for success
- God blesses the rich abundantly to help the needy; do not hoard God's blessings in your hands
- When the righteous and honest rule, the people will rejoice

THE LION WHO ASKED FOR TOO MUCH

O nce upon a time, a lion king made a proclamation throughout all the animal kingdom. He summoned all the animals to a meeting in front of his den.

"In view of the fact that I am the present royal majesty of this kingdom, I cannot be expected to be running after you all in search of my meal. Therefore, I hereby make a decree that henceforth, all the animals will have to come to my den willingly.

This will help me to concentrate my energy on the demanding task of ruling this vast animal kingdom. I have instructed all my aides to make a timetable to that effect."

So, the King's guard read out a roaster of animals to be used for meal by the king and the time they would be eaten. The animals became scared and greatly troubled. One by one, they went to present themselves to the great lion whenever it was their turn to be devoured by him. One day, it was the turn of the tortoise. The lion waited and waited for his meal, but the tortoise did not turn up. The lion was enraged and promised to send his aides –the hyenas- to punish the offender with torture before eating him. Suddenly, the tortoise appeared from nowhere.

"Why did you keep me waiting? I have not eaten since morning, and you are just coming by this time!" The lion roared.

The tortoise, lowering his head replied, "I'm sorry for arriving here later than expected, your majesty, but it was not my fault. I was on my way here at the right time. But on my way, I saw a lion as big as yourself who told me he was the one I was to offer myself to."

"What? An impostor in my kingdom?"

"The lion also informed me that he is now the king of the forest. That from now onwards, no animal should come to your den any longer. He further asked me to call you for a fight to prove who the stronger lion is and the rightful leader in this forest. He flexed his muscles and promised to destroy you if you dared show your ugly face."

"What impudence?" the lion roared in anger.

"He also said that if I told you this, you would back off him and that cowards like you often run away from fights."

The lion was visibly angry and roared again, angrier than they had ever seen him.

"Take me to this foolish lion, now!"

"I advise you, your majesty, to avoid this powerful lion. Please avoid trouble."

"No! Take me to him now."

So, the tortoise led the way and the fuming lion followed him into the thicket. The journey was slow and this made the lion angrier than ever. At last, the tortoise led the lion to a well and asked permission to stay away from the fight.

"Where is the fool that dared challenge my authority? Show me the impostor immediately."

"He lives inside that place, my king."

The tortoise pointed at the well. In anger, the lion went near the well and looked in. He was amazed to see the other lion looking straight at him. He roared and the lion in the well also roared at him.

So, the lion charged and jumped into the well, where he drowned and died. The rest of the animals crowned the tortoise as the new king of the forest in recognition of his efforts at delivering them from the tyranny of the old lion.

Moral lessons

One should not enjoy the privilege of leadership at the expense of followers. Privileged positions should not be abused.

ABOUT THE AUTHOR

Feyi Oluwasanmi is a seasoned servant of God. As a pastor and evangelist, he has been permitted by grace to be involved in leadership positions in the Christian body since 1984. He holds a B. Agric (Hons), PGDM in General Management, a Masters in Business Administration (Marketing), and a certificate in Computer Networking.

He rose to become the President of the Gospel Students' Fellowship (Obafemi Awolowo University Chapter). He was the Prayer Secretary of Nigerian Christian Corpers' Fellowship, Kano state during his national service year.

He founded the Fishermen Ministry International- a ministry devoted majorly to the intercession, evangelism, and deliverance of souls. He also leads the Christ Image Foundation.

The author- a former senior staff in a bank- is now a faculty member in a business academy, where he lectures on Business Systems Development and Management of Small-Scale Enterprises; he also doubles up as an environmental consultant with deep interest in waste management, wildlife protection, pollution control, occupational safety, and environmental and social impact assessment

He is a prolific writer whose work has featured in magazines, devotionals, and journals. He is a member and certified trainer in Dynamic Church Planters International, USA. Feyi is also an alumnus of the Haggai Institute for Advanced Leadership.

He is married to Ijeoma and the union is blessed with four children. 'Seun, 'Damilola, Ibukun and Ayanfe. He lives in Akure, Ondo State of Nigeria from where he travels around preaching the full gospel with accompanying signs and wonders.

THE END

FEYI OLUWASANMI

FEYI OLUWASANMI

FEYI OLUWASANMI

www.ingramcontent.com/pod-product-compliance
Lightning Source LLC
Chambersburg PA
CBHW050309260626
47156CB00005B/1724